ROBERT AND GREAT GRANNY

Every Christmas Great Granny comes to stay at Robert's house. Great Granny is very old and her legs don't work well any more so that she can't climb the stairs. But she has lots of wonderful stories to tell Robert, all about the things that happened to her when she was just a little girl.

Also by Anne Rooke
in Magnet Books

When Robert Went to Play Group

Anne Rooke

Robert and Great Granny

Illustrated by Lesley Smith

A Magnet Book

For my parents and Tante

First published in 1986
by Hodder and Stoughton Ltd
This Magnet edition first published in 1987
by Methuen Children's Books Ltd
11 New Fetter Lane, London EC4P 4EE
Text copyright © 1986 Anne Rooke
Illustrations copyright © 1986 Hodder and Stoughton Ltd
Printed in Great Britain
by Richard Clay Ltd, Bungay, Suffolk

ISBN 0 416 01302 3

Contents

Fetching Great Granny

Every Christmas Great Granny came to stay at Robert's house.

Great Granny was very old and her legs didn't work well any more so that she couldn't climb stairs. Robert's father said, 'If Great Granny can't go upstairs to bed she'll just have to go downstairs to bed.' And that is what she did.

Near the front door of Robert's house there was a small room. Robert's family kept coats and boots in there. They also kept garden chairs, a sewing machine, a typewriter and a tall set of drawers called a filing cabinet full of important papers.

But, a week before Christmas, Robert's mother and father cleared all these things out of the small room and put them in other corners of the house. Then they carried the spare bed out of Robert's bedroom and humped it down the stairs – bump, bump, bump. And they set it up again in the small room by the front door. They put sheets and blankets and a red eiderdown on the bed and a red and blue carpet on the floor. Robert carried down the white table from beside his bed and his mother looked in the cupboard under the stairs for a lamp. Robert asked his mother for the kitchen scissors and he took them out into the garden. There weren't many flowers in the garden so near to Christmas, but he did find two pink rose buds and three yellow pansies. He put them in an old peanut-butter jar and filled it up with water. He put the flowers on Great Granny's bedside table beside the lamp.

The next day was a Sunday. Robert and his father drove all the way to London and went to Great Granny's flat. They went up in a lift and stopped with a bump at Great Granny's floor.

'Just push the door,' called Great Granny when Robert pressed her doorbell. 'Come in quickly and let me look at you.'

Robert's father pushed open the door and went in. Robert stood in the hall near the lift because he felt shy.

'Where is he? Where's that great grandson of mine?' said Great Granny, coming slowly to the front door. She looked out into the hall near the lift. 'He's vanished,' she said. 'He must be magic.'

'Oh no, I'm not,' Robert shouted, jumping up and down. 'I'm not vanished. I'm here.'

'What a good thing,' said Great Granny, 'or I would have had to throw the flapjacks to the birds.'

'I like flapjacks,' said Robert.

'Then you'd better come in and eat them,' said Great Granny. 'Before your father has them all.'

So Robert went in to Great Granny's flat and ate four flapjacks and had a cup of tea, just like the grown-ups.

Some time later Robert's father carried Great

Granny's big brown suitcase down to the street outside the block of flats and put it in the back of the car. He went up again in the lift and carried down two large cardboard boxes. Great Granny put on her coat and hat and hung her bag around her neck. Robert got the two long steel sticks with curving leather bits at the top which Great Granny kept by her front door to help her walk when she went out. Then Great Granny took her keys off a hook in the kitchen and said, 'Robert, you look a sensible chap to me. Could you take these keys and ring Mrs Hargreaves's door bell just down the corridor? Then say "These are my Great Granny's keys." Can you do that, please?'

'Yes,' said Robert, taking the keys and going to ring the next-door bell.

Mrs Hargreaves was a very kind lady and she came out of her flat and told Great Granny that she would lock up for her and keep an eye on things while she was away.

Then Robert and Great Granny went down in the lift and Great Granny let him press the buttons and open the door.

It took a long time to help Great Granny into the car. Her legs were so stiff they wouldn't bend at all but Robert's father managed to lift her into the front seat and Robert did up her seat belt for her – clunk–click. Then Robert climbed

into the back of the car and they drove off.

'Now I feel Christmas has really begun,' said Great Granny.

It was after Robert's bed-time when they got home. His little sister Susan had been in bed for a long time. He had a cheese sandwich and a drink of milk. He ate his apple while he was in the bath. His mother was busy talking to Great Granny. Robert got out of the bath and dried himself a bit and put on his pyjamas. When he went downstairs he said, 'When can I have my story?'

But his mother said, 'Robert, it is after eight o'clock. It's high time you were in bed. Now, say goodnight to Great Granny and off you go.'

Great Granny said, 'Goodnight, Robert dear. Thank you for coming to fetch me.'

Robert kissed her and said, 'Two stories tomorrow.'

'All right,' said Great Granny. 'Two stories. Sleep well.'

The Breakfast Story

The next morning Robert's father went off to work after breakfast. When Robert and Susan had finished their breakfasts their mother said, 'Now, I'll get Great Granny's breakfast.'

She put a tray on the kitchen table and a white cloth on the tray. Then she got out a cup and saucer and plate.

'Could you find me a small knife and a small spoon, please, dear?' she said to Robert.

Robert got them out of the drawer in the kitchen table and watched while his mother spooned some marmalade into one white bowl and some butter into another. She cut two slices of brown bread and put them on the plate. Then she filled a small teapot with boiling water from the kettle and put some milk into a jug.

'What else?' she said.

'She likes a cloth to wipe her fingers,' said Robert.

'So she does, Robert,' said his mother. 'Did

you remember that from last year?'

Robert nodded.

His mother picked up the tray and carried it to the small room by the front door. She knocked on the door and said, 'Breakfast's coming, Granny.'

Great Granny was awake, propped up on three pillows. She couldn't sit up more than that because she wasn't bendy in the middle any more. Robert's mother put the tray on Great Granny's lap. 'Did you sleep well?' she said.

'Beautifully,' said Great Granny. 'And what a lovely breakfast. Did you get it for me, Robert?'

'Bits of it,' said Robert. 'I can help you if you like.'

'That's just what I would like,' said Great Granny. 'Thank you,' she said to Robert's mother.

Robert stayed beside Great Granny's bed and carefully poured a little milk into her cup. Great Granny poured out the tea because that was so hot it was dangerous.

'This knife isn't dangerous,' said Robert. 'I can spread your butter and marmalade for you.'

'Thank you,' said Great Granny.

The butter was rather cold and hard and when Robert tried to spread it it made holes in the soft bread. He looked at Great Granny. 'I can stick it together again with the marmalade,' he said.

'Yes, of course,' said Great Granny. 'Perhaps
that's what marmalade is for.'

So Robert did his best to mend the pieces of
bread and Great Granny popped a lump of bread,
butter and marmalade into her mouth. 'It's very
good,' she said. 'You try some.'

Robert ate the messiest lump. It was very
good. 'It's a good thing I remembered that cloth
to wipe us with,' he said.

'Isn't it just,' said Great Granny. 'Did your mother make this good marmalade?'

Robert shook his head. 'We buy it in the shop,' he said.

'Very wise,' said Great Granny. 'Years ago when I was your mother's age I used to make marmalade every year after Christmas. But I stopped.'

'Why?' Robert asked, having another messy piece of bread.

'Because one day when I was putting oranges into a saucepan my son James heaved a great big sigh and do you know what he said?'

Robert shook his head.

'He said, "Now you'll have a cross face all day." Well, I said, "You make it then, James." And that's just what he did. He was older than you, so it wasn't very dangerous. And he made lovely marmalade. My marmalade was a bit tricky. Sometimes it was so runny it slid off the toast. Sometimes it was so stiff it was hard to get it out of the jar. But James's marmalade was always just right. So every year after Christmas he made the marmalade. And when he grew up and left home and couldn't make it any more I used to buy mine at a shop, just like your mother does. And so we *never* have cross faces, do we?'

Robert looked at Great Granny's face and saw her looking at him very crossly.

'Yes, you do,' he said laughing.

'Oh no, I don't,' said Great Granny, frowning. And then her face changed and she smiled. 'And when James grew up do you know what he became?'

Robert shook his head.

'He became your Grandad.'

'My Grandad?'

'That's right,' said Great Granny. 'And when you next see him you ask him to make you some marmalade.'

Robert nodded.

'And he can make some for me too,' Great Granny added, looking at her plate. 'You seem to have eaten most of mine.'

The Fine Moustache

Great Granny spent all that first morning at Robert's house getting dressed and sorting out her room. She put two photographs in frames beside the flowers and lamp on her bedside table. She hung her dresses and skirts and blouses on hangers on the pegs around the wall of her small bedroom. She put her hairbrush and comb, a blue bottle of lavender water and a white box of face powder on the window-sill. There was a small wash-basin in the corner of the room and on that she put her orange flannel and a piece of special pink soap which she had had for her birthday.

When Robert came into her room to tell her it was lunch time he said, 'I like this room better now.'

Then he went to look at the photographs on the table. One was the face of a man with a great big fair moustache. Great Granny saw him looking at the man and said, 'That's my

husband. He's your Great Grandfather.'

'Has he died now?' Robert asked.

'Yes, he died a long time ago. And shall I tell you what his name was?'

Robert nodded.

'It was Robert – just like you,' said Great Granny. 'And do you see the way his eyes crinkle at the corners?'

Robert looked and saw the way Great Grandfather's eyes went up at the ends.

'Well,' said Great Granny, 'Your eyes do just the same. It's quite amazing how like him you are.'

After that Robert looked at the photograph even more carefully.

While Great Granny pulled the eiderdown straight on her bed Robert looked at the other photograph. 'Who's that?' he asked.

'That's my mother. Your Great-great Granny. Just think of that.'

'She looks a bit sad,' said Robert.

'Yes, I suppose she does,' said Great Granny. 'But you see, in those days, people had to sit still for a long time to have their photographs taken. So that's why they look sad. They were frightened of blinking or sneezing. She wasn't always sad at all.'

'Mummy says it's lunch-time,' said Robert, remembering why he had come.

'Oh, my goodness,' said Great Granny. 'Pass me those sticks by the door and you scuttle along.'

But Robert ran off upstairs.

When Great Granny was sitting comfortably by the kitchen table ready to have lunch, Robert's mother strapped Susan into her high chair and said, 'Where's Robert?'

'Here I am,' said Robert, coming into the kitchen.

Everybody looked at him because his voice sounded funny. And then they saw why, and Great Granny burst out laughing, and Susan jumped up and down and made her chair wobble.

Robert had got a ball of cotton wool out of Susan's changing basket and had stuck it under his nose with some of her Vaseline.

'What a fine moustache,' said Great Granny. 'I have never seen a child look so like his Great Grandfather.'

'Once his beard grows he'll look like Father Christmas,' said Robert's mother.

But Robert was looking at his plate of shepherd's pie and carrots. 'I'll have to take it off when I eat things,' he said.

'Perhaps Father Christmas does too,' said Great Granny. 'He seems a sensible chap – like you.'

The Donkey Mower

After lunch Great Granny went to sit in a comfortable chair by the fire. Robert's mother fetched a low stool for her to rest her legs on and Robert got a tartan rug from his bedroom and put it over Great Granny's legs.

'That's lovely,' said Great Granny. 'I'm as snug as a bug in a rug.'

Susan tried to say that but she couldn't.

'Now,' said Robert's mother as she picked up Susan. 'It's time for Granny and Susan to have their rests. Come along, Robert, we'll leave Granny in peace.'

So Robert went to play with his box of Lego on the kitchen floor and his mother carried Susan up to her cot.

For a while Robert played happily. Then he looked in his box for one of his Lego men to go in the car he was making. It wasn't there. And then Robert remembered where he had left it. It was under the chair which Great Granny was sitting on. There were several farm animals under there too, Robert remembered. Susan had put them under the chair when she tried to join in his game.

Very quietly Robert opened the sitting room door and looked inside. Great Granny had the newspaper over her lap and her eyes were shut. Robert tip-toed across the room and began to rummage under her chair. Suddenly he jumped.

'And what have you got there?' said Great Granny.

'A Lego man and a sheep and a donkey,' said Robert. 'I thought you were asleep.'

'How can I sleep with a Lego man, a sheep and a donkey under my chair?' Great Granny asked.

Robert laughed. 'They aren't real,' he said. 'They're just toys. I haven't got a *real* donkey.'

'I did,' said Great Granny.

'When?' said Robert.

'When I was about your age. He was called Johnny Jones. I *did* love him.'

'What did he look like?' asked Robert.

'Well, he was a little white donkey with darker legs and dark tips to his ears. His head was very big and his hoofs were very small. His hoofs were his feet.'

'I know that,' said Robert.

'But what you don't know,' said Great

Granny, 'was that he used to wear brown leather shoes. They were made of the stuff your lace-up shoes are made of.'

Robert thought for a while. 'I've never seen a donkey in shoes like that. There's a donkey at Mr Mummery's farm. We have to go and see her a lot because Susan likes her. But she doesn't wear shoes like that.'

'No, I'm sure she doesn't,' said Great Granny. 'But Johnny Jones had to because he used to mow the grass. You see, when I was a little girl I lived in a house with a big garden. There was a long lawn which stretched down to a river. And, in those days, we didn't have motor mowers to cut the grass, we had Johnny Jones instead. My father used to strap a big cutting machine, with blades that went round and round, behind Johnny Jones and he would pull it, up and down, up and down, up to the house and down to the river, he pulled that cutting machine until all the grass was cut. And, because my father didn't want his little hoofs to make holes in the lawn, he made Johnny Jones four brown leather shoes which did up around his legs with laces. We always laughed when we saw him wearing them.'

And Great Granny and Robert were quiet for a moment, thinking about Johnny Jones's leather shoes.

Then Great Granny said, 'But one day a terrible thing happened. I was playing in the garden with my big brother George, and Johnny Jones was walking up and down cutting the grass. Quite suddenly he stopped and looked across at us on the other side of the garden. My father usually walked up and down with the donkey, but just then he was standing a little way behind him, lighting his pipe. I think Johnny Jones looked at us and wondered if we had any sugar lumps for him, because he waggled his ears and trotted very quickly across the garden towards us, pulling his grass cutter – rattly-clank. And between us and him there was a beautiful flower-bed. It was full of geraniums and snapdragons and blue lobelia and white alyssum – all my mother's favourite flowers. And Johnny Jones trotted straight through the lot – trit, trot, rattle, clank, cut, cut, cut. Well, you can imagine what a mess he made of the lovely flower-bed. And we children shouted and my father *roared*. So poor Johnny Jones thought he'd

better turn round and go back. And he dragged
the mower round in a circle, quite finishing off
the poor flower bed. My father clutched at his
halter and pulled him off on to the grass again.
We looked at the flower bed – all trampled and
mangled – and George said, "What will Mother
say?" And that made Father even crosser.'

'What *did* your mother say?' Robert asked.

'Well, it's a funny thing,' said Great Granny.
'But Mother had seen what happened from an
upstairs window. And she came out into the
garden laughing and laughing and saying how
funny Johnny Jones and Father had looked.'

'So it was all right,' said Robert.

'I'm afraid it made Father crosser than ever,'
said Great Granny. 'George and I had to pick up
all the poor cut and squashed flowers and put
them in vases in the house. And I seem to remember that after that George had the job of
minding Johnny Jones's grass cutting.'

'I don't suppose he smoked a pipe,' said
Robert.

'No, I don't suppose he did,' said Great
Granny.

Robert looked at the little toy donkey in his
hand and said, 'Can I bring my Lego in here to
play with, in case you remember more things
about Johnny Jones?'

'Yes, do,' said Great Granny.

So Robert carried his Lego box in from the kitchen, and played with it until it was time for children's television. But although he clattered the Lego a lot, Great Granny went sound asleep and didn't wake up until tea-time.

More Cutting

'You look very clean and shiny,' Great Granny said when Robert came downstairs after his bath that evening.

'Susan's having her hair shampooed,' Robert said. 'I told Mummy I would come and talk to you instead.'

'I see,' said Great Granny. 'Do you like having your hair washed?'

'It's all right,' Robert said. 'I lie down backwards in the bath and do it myself. That's best. How do you do yours?'

'Well,' said Great Granny, 'I lie backwards too, with the back of my neck on the edge of a wash-basin. A kind girl called Debbie shampoos it for me. But when I was a little girl having my hair washed was a terrible palaver. That means a terrible fuss.'

'Why?' asked Robert.

'I had so much of it, for a start,' said Great Granny. 'And then our mother said that we had to have it washed in pure rain-water.'

'Where did you get that from?' Robert asked.

'Out of the rain-water butt in the garden. There was a big barrel with pipes leading down to it from the roof of the house. And we washed our hair in the water from that to make it soft and silky.'

'Did your big brother George?' asked Robert.

'I shouldn't think so, would you?' Great Granny said. 'But how I wished I had short hair like him. No bother. No trouble. I don't remember him even combing his much. My hair went right down to my bottom. I could sit on it – if I put my head back, that is.'

Robert nodded and pulled at his own hair to see how long it would stretch. He could just see the front bit if he looked up hard.

'And then, one hot day in summer, I got really cross with my hair. It was always being plaited and pinned or else it got in my way. We had been paddling in the little river I told you about at the end of our garden. And my plaits of hair got all wet at the ends. George said, "I don't know why you don't chop the silly things off. I would." And, because it was just what I was wishing I could do, I jumped out of the river and ran across the grass and into the house. I went straight to Mother's work-basket where she kept her scissors and I grabbed hold of one of my plaits with one hand and I opened her great scissors with the other and I went *snip*.'

Robert looked at Great Granny. He knew it was bad to take grown–ups' scissors. 'Oh dear,' he said.

'I'm afraid it was oh dear,' Great Granny agreed. 'Because the scissors only went some of

the way through my great thick plait and I had to hack and hack to get it off. Then I set about the other plait. When that was off, I picked them both up and ran back to George. And I can remember now how light and funny my head felt – rather like your feet do when you've taken off some heavy boots. I ran back to George holding up my plaits for him to see. "Now you've done it," he said. "Now you've done it." '

'What did your mother say about the scissors?' Robert asked.

'I can't remember her saying anything about those,' Great Granny said. 'But I do remember what Father said. He said, "Why is that child wearing a hat all the time?" You see, I had put on an old woolly hat of Mother's to hide my short hair. And it was summer time so it must have looked rather odd. Well, I think I was rather brave. I said, "Because I've cut off my hair," and I took off the hat. And my poor father sat down and looked at me – and looked at me – until I ran over and hugged him and said I would never do it again.'

'Did you ever do it again?' Robert asked.

'Luckily Debbie cuts it for me now – and makes a far better job of it.'

Just then they heard Robert's mother and Susan coming down the stairs. Robert looked at his Great Granny. 'I won't tell Mummy about you taking those scissors,' he whispered.

Great Granny nodded. 'Best to keep that under your hat,' she whispered back.

Later that evening Robert went and stood beside Great Granny's chair, holding a story book.

'Have you come to say goodnight?' Great Granny asked.

Robert shook his head slowly. 'Last night you said I could have two stories tonight.'

'I'm afraid you'll have to ask your mummy or daddy to read those to you,' said Great Granny. 'My eyes don't work well enough any more. All my stories are in my head.'

'That's all right,' said Robert. 'I like head stories. Are there any more?'

'Loads of them,' said Great Granny. 'But tomorrow I want *you* to tell *me* some.'

'Yes,' said Robert. 'That's fair.'

Bad Luck

The next morning Robert watched his mother getting the breakfast tray ready for Great Granny again. He fetched the knife and spoon and got two white bowls out of the cupboard as well. Then he picked up the marmalade jar.

'It's all gone,' Robert said.

His mother looked at the empty jar. 'But it was half full,' she said. 'Where can it have all gone?'

'Dad had it on his toast,' Robert said. Then he added, 'I did too,' because his mother's face looked rather cross.

His mother opened the larder door and looked along the shelves.

'She might like peanut butter,' Robert said.

But his mother had got down a purplish-red jar of something.

'The year before last's damson jam,' she said. 'Well, let's see what it's like.' She took off the shiny paper on top of the jar and dug a spoon

into the jam. She tasted it and said, 'It seems all right. You try some,' and she gave Robert the spoon to lick.

'It's lovely,' said Robert. 'Great Granny will like that a lot.'

So his mother got out another spoon and emptied some of the damson jam into a white bowl and put it on the tray. When everything was ready she carried it through to Great Granny in her small bedroom.

'Can you stay and help me again?' Great Granny asked Robert when she had the tray on her lap.

'I think I can,' said Robert and he poured the milk into Great Granny's cup again.

'Is this plum jam?' Great Granny asked, looking closely at the white bowl.

'No, it's not,' said Robert, trying to remember. 'It's called something else.'

Suddenly Great Granny said in an excited sort of voice, 'It's not *damson* jam, is it?'

'Yes, that's right,' said Robert happily. 'It's damson jam. I remembered.'

'It's years and years since I've had damson jam. Your Great Grandfather –'

'The one called Robert,' said Robert.

'That's the one,' agreed Great Granny. 'Well, he would never have it in the house. He said it was bad luck.'

'Is it?' said Robert looking hard at the jam on the tray.

'No, of course not,' said Great Granny laughing. 'It was just because of something that happened when he was a little boy.'

'Was he very little?' Robert asked.

'More middling, I suppose. Shall I tell you about it?'

Robert nodded.

'Let me think. Now, when Great Grandfather Robert was a middling boy he had a brother called John and sometimes they used to have a little pocket money. Do you have pocket money?'

'Yes. I had some to buy you a Christmas

present. I got you a –' said Robert stopping
suddenly. 'I mustn't tell you,' he said.

'Or I won't have a surprise,' Great Granny
said. 'But Robert and John had a surprise all
right. You see they took their pocket money to
the shop near their house. And in the shop was
a big box of damsons. They looked at the purple
shiny damsons like little plums, and, my word,
they did look good. So they spent all their pocket
money – every bit – on a great big brown paper
bag full of damsons. They did not buy any
chocolate or toffee or humbugs – nothing – just
damsons. And then they walked down the road
back to their home. Well, on the way they
opened the bag and each boy took out a damson
and popped it in his mouth – like that.'

And then Great Granny's whole face screwed
up and her mouth turned down at the corners.
And Robert's face did the same as he watched
her.

'Yes, you've guessed,' said Great Granny.
'Those damsons were as sour as sour as could
be. Real little horrors. And those poor boys had
spent all their money on them. They *were* cross.
And do you know what they did?'

Robert frowned. 'Did they put sugar on
them?' he asked.

'That would have been a very good idea.
But no, I'm afraid they didn't do anything so

sensible. They did a very silly thing. They were walking along beside a high garden wall. And your Great Grandfather was so angry about the sour damsons that he stood still and threw the bag up, up and over the wall. But at once they heard a great shout from the other side of the wall and those boys began to run. They ran and

ran until they were safely back in their own garden.'

'Good,' said Robert, flopping on to the end of Great Granny's bed.

'I'm sorry to say,' said Great Granny pouring some tea into her cup, 'that the person who gave that great shout – aaahr – like that – jumped up on his side of the wall and saw the two boys running away and *knew who they were*. Later on that day the shouter came to see your Great Grandfather's mother and father and said the two boys were a disgrace and ought to be punished. And certainly it is not a good thing to throw bags of damsons over walls – especially when they land on people's heads – I'm sure you never do. So poor Robert and John had no more pocket money for a very long time. And after that Robert would never eat a damson, even when it was made into jam with heaps of sugar. And so I didn't eat them much either.'

'You can have all this pot if you like,' said Robert. 'I won't have any.'

'That is very kind of you,' said Great Granny. 'But years and years afterwards my son James –'

'That's Grandad,' said Robert.

'Yes, Grandad – he had a garden with a damson tree in it and when I went to stay with him I had lovely damson jam.'

And then Robert remembered. 'We get our

damsons from Grandad's tree. He brings us lots and lots. Mummy says, "Bother, I'll have to make jam. Bother." '

Great Granny laughed. 'I used to feel like that too. But, of course, James never dared give me damsons because his father would have said, "Take the nasty things away. They are bad luck." '

'I'll tell Mummy that,' said Robert.

'You'll save her a lot of trouble,' said Great Granny. 'Just you tell her what to say when Grandad comes with a load of them.'

'Aaarh – damsons! Bad luck!' yelled Robert.

Christmas Shopping

'I need you to help me this afternoon,' Robert's mother said.

'Yes, I'll do that,' said Robert.

'Granny has to do her Christmas shopping. We can take her into town this afternoon. And one of the big shops will let us borrow a wheel-chair for her.'

'Can I push it?' Robert asked.

'I don't think you are tall enough,' said his mother. 'But it would be a great help if you pushed Susan's pushchair. Could you do that?'

Robert said nothing. He was used to pushing Susan around, so it wasn't exciting any more.

Great Granny and Robert's mother took a long time getting ready to go shopping. Susan and Robert stood by the front door all ready to go out while Great Granny made sure she had everything she needed and Robert's mother put a hot water bottle on the front seat of the car.

But, at last, Robert and Susan were belted into their places in the back seat of the car and Great Granny began to get into the car as well. Robert's mother pulled Great Granny into the car and then ran around to help her legs in and then back again to make her straight. Lastly she did up Great Granny's safety belt.

'I'm sitting on something hot,' said Great Granny as they drove off towards the town.

'Good heavens, yes,' said Robert's mother. 'I left the hot water bottle on the seat.'

'It's lovely,' said Great Granny. 'I must sit on one more often. Just so long as it doesn't burst.'

Robert's mother was allowed to park the car right outside the big shop in town and a kind man came out of the shop pushing a wheelchair. He was able to help Great Granny out of the car and into the wheelchair in no time at all.

'Now, if you park your car behind the store, madam,' he said to Robert's mother, 'we'll look after this lady until you come.'

So Robert stayed with Great Granny while his mother drove the car around the corner.

'My great grandson would like to try pushing me,' Great Granny explained to the kind man from the shop. 'Would that be all right?'

The man looked at Robert. 'Very gently now, young man,' he said. 'Remember it's not a toboggan.'

So Robert held the handle at the back of Great Granny's chair and gave it a push.

'Whee,' said Great Granny. 'This is the life.'

'I'm here, madam,' said the kind man. 'I'll make sure you're all right.'

Robert pushed Great Granny through the enormous glass doors and into the shop. The man held the doors open for him and then walked along beside Great Granny because Robert wasn't tall enough to see where he was pushing.

'Watch out,' said the man suddenly. 'Sorry, ladies,' he said to some shoppers as Great Granny's wheelchair brushed past them.

'Perhaps I had better take over, young man,' he said to Robert.

'My great grandson is doing fine. I'll shoo

people out of the way as we go,' said Great
Granny. And she called, 'Excuse us. May we
come past?' to some people who got out of her
way at once.

'Where would you like to go, madam?' the
man asked.

'The toy department, please,' Great Granny
said.

'Then we must take the lift to the third floor,'
said the man.

'Oh, good,' said Great Granny.

When they reached the lift Robert ran forward
and pushed the button with an arrow on it
pointing upwards. 'Ding,' said the lift as the
doors opened and Great Granny let the kind man
push her safely into the lift.

'Robert, I need your help,' said Great Granny as the lift went upwards. 'What would Susan like for Christmas?'

'She wants a swimming pool,' said Robert.

'Oh dear,' said Great Granny. 'This shop doesn't sell them.'

Robert thought again. 'She likes those bubbles you blow. But she mustn't drink the stuff,' he said.

At that moment the lift went 'ding' again and the door opened. There in front of them was the toy department with beautiful tinselly lights and stars hung across it and Christmas music playing and piles of dolls and cars and paints and models and jigsaws and games. Robert walked out and looked around. Then he remembered Great Granny, but luckily the man had pushed her chair out of the lift before the door shut again.

'I think Susan likes everything here,' he said to Great Granny.

Great Granny nodded. 'What about an easy jigsaw?' she said. And the man pushed her wheelchair towards the jigsaws. Robert ran on in front to look. But on the way he saw a badger. It was not a big badger. It was far smaller than the teddy bears and dolls it was sitting with. In fact it was being rather squashed by a large pink bear with a blue bow which was flopping over it so that the badger's stripy face looked out a little sadly. Robert went over to it and touched its small black nose. Great Granny headed on towards the jigsaws. Robert pushed the pink bear off the badger and stroked its back. Then he went to join Great Granny.

'We've got some of those jigsaws at play group,' he said.

'Show me which ones you haven't got and we'll choose one for Susan,' said Great Granny.

Robert looked carefully. 'They're all too difficult,' he said. 'It'll have to be bubble stuff.'

'What about that toy you were looking at just now, by the teddies?'

'No,' said Robert quickly. 'She might bash it. She does.'

'Then let's get her a hammering set.'

Robert nodded. 'Do it now. Before Mummy gets here.'

An assistant wrapped up a hammering set with coloured pegs and Great Granny got out her purse. Just then Robert's mother arrived, pushing Susan in her pushchair.

'Here you are,' she said. 'No, Susan, don't grab at things. No, you don't want that pink teddy. Robert, could you push Susan down among the train sets? She may not clutch at those.'

So Robert pushed Susan down the shop and around the pile of Lego boxes and back to Great Granny.

'There, I've finished. How about a lovely scarf for you, my dear?' Great Granny said to Robert's mother.

'I would love one. There are some beauties downstairs,' said Robert's mother guiding the wheelchair back towards the lift.

And, as he pushed Susan after them, Robert noticed that Great Granny was now holding *two* parcels on her lap.

Car Rides

'This is a lovely warm car,' said Great Granny as they drove home from the town later that afternoon. 'We used to have to wrap up so much to go motoring. And then the car was always breaking down.'

'Can you remember your first trip in a car?' Robert's mother asked.

'Yes, indeed,' said Great Granny. 'And it was nearly my last.'

'Did George go?' Robert asked from his place in the back of the car.

'What did you say, dear?' Great Granny called.

'Did – George – go?' Robert shouted.

'No, he didn't. I'll tell you about it when we get home.'

But when they got home Robert's mother made Great Granny a cup of tea and Robert watched television while Susan went to sleep under the kitchen table. It wasn't until bed-time that

Robert remembered Great Granny had promised to tell him a story. So he went and stood beside her chair in the sitting room. Her eyes were shut so he leaned forward and said in her ear, 'Are you asleep, Great Granny?'

'Yes,' said Great Granny.

'Can you tell me your story now?'

'Why don't _you_ tell me one instead?'

'Do you know the one about the three bears?' Robert asked. Great Granny shook her head.

Robert sighed. 'It's not very interesting,' he said. 'Yours are better.'

Great Granny opened her eyes and yawned. 'Dear me,' she said. 'Now, what was I going to tell you about?'

'When you went in a car and George didn't,' said Robert.

'Ah, yes,' said Great Granny slowly. 'Well, when I was a little girl I had a friend called Mary. Mary lived in a big house near mine and we used to play together a lot. One day I was playing at Mary's house when her father came in all jolly and bright, rubbing his hands together and smiling broadly. "Come and see what I've got," he said. "Just you come and see." Mary and I ran after him, down the stairs and out on to their front door step. And there was the most beautiful – guess what –'

'Car,' said Robert.

'That's right. I had seen pictures of motor cars but I had never seen a real one before. It was silver all over with huge headlights – quite beautiful. And Mary's father went down the steps and stood beside it, stroking it and talking to it. Then he turned to Mary and me and said, "What are we waiting for? Let's go for a ride. Come along."

'And in no time at all we were squeezing into the back seat. Mary's father turned a handle in the front of the car and it began to jolt and shudder. I was a bit scared but Mary's father shouted, "Hang on, ladies," and jumped into the driving seat. We roared out of their drive and bounced along the village street. I had never been in anything so *fast* and I'm afraid I was so scared I began to cry. But, of course, Mary's father couldn't see and he began to sing. Suddenly the vicar came round the corner driving his pony and trap. "Shoo! Out of the way, Vicar," Mary's father shouted and the vicar's pony nearly fell down with fright. And then we saw a lady pushing a pram. "Look out, we're coming," shouted Mary's father, thinking it was all a great joke. And then I saw that the lady pushing the pram was *my* mother pushing *my* baby brother straight into the hedge. And I began to cry even harder. My mother pulled the pram angrily out of the hedge and waved her fist – like this – at our car. And then she saw me

sitting in the back and her hand flew to her mouth and she looked *horrified*.'

'Horrified. Horrified,' said Robert because it was such a fine word.

'As we turned a corner in the road I saw my mother running back down the village street pushing my baby brother at a great rate. On we went over the hill to the main road. And I stopped crying and began to enjoy myself. You see, wherever we went, everyone ran out of the houses and waved and shouted at us. And I felt so grand that it was good fun to shout back and cheer. We didn't stop once until we were back in Mary's drive. And then we found that Mary's father wasn't very good at stopping. We shot straight across the grass and into a hedge before we stopped. Then Mary's father jumped out of the car and saw my mother standing at the top of the front steps. And my word, she was cross. She said he was never, never to take her daughter out in that dangerous motor car again. And what did he think he was doing frightening the countryside.'

'She was very horrified,' said Robert.

'That's right, she was,' Great Granny agreed. 'And she took me straight home and told Father all about it.'

'What did Father say?' Robert asked.

'He said, "What? Has Mary's father got a

motor? Lucky devil! I wish we had one." '

'Did he get one?' Robert asked.

Great Granny shook her head. 'Not until we children were all grown-ups. But I'll tell you a secret.'

'What?' Robert asked.

'Sometimes he used to go over to Mary's house and go for a drive with Mary's father. The vicar saw him driving the car one day and said he was even more dangerous than Mary's father.'

'Like you in your wheelchair,' Robert said.

'I beg your pardon, young man,' said Great Granny very grandly. 'I am not dangerous.'

'Those ladies in the shop said you were,' said Robert.

'And who was pushing me?' Great Granny asked.

Robert laughed. 'I was,' he said.

'Next time,' said Great Granny, 'we'll have to take a hooter.'

Two Rosies

The next morning the two little girls from next door came to play at Robert's house. Their mother was going shopping and Robert's mother said she would look after them for her. Rosie was Robert's friend and Daisy was Susan's friend.

Susan and Daisy played in the kitchen. They emptied out a cupboard full of clattery saucepans. Robert's mother was cooking and pretended not to mind the noise. But Robert said to Rosie, 'Let's go and play somewhere else.' And Rosie said, 'Yes. Those two are making too much noise.'

So Robert and Rosie went upstairs to play with the toys in Robert's bedroom.

Suddenly Robert said, 'I've got a Great Granny downstairs.'

Rosie said, 'What's a Great Granny?' Because, although she had a granny, she had never heard of a Great Granny.

'D'you want to see?' Robert asked.

Rosie nodded, though she wasn't sure if she wanted to or not. She followed Robert downstairs and watched while he went to the door of Great Granny's room. He knocked at the door.

'Who's there?' Great Granny called.

'Me,' said Robert.

'Ah, come in, Me,' said Great Granny. And Robert opened the door and went in.

'You're just in time to help me,' Great Granny said. 'Could you pull this stocking up for me? I can't bend down far enough, you see.'

Robert pulled Great Granny's stocking up her leg for her.

'That's marvellous,' said Great Granny. Then she picked up a very strange thing. It was like a great big pair of scissors and when she squeezed

the handles two fingers shot out in a criss-cross so that she could pick things up without bending. She picked up the other stocking with the special criss-cross thing and rolled it back. She gave the stocking to Robert to pull over her toes.

'Can I have a go with that criss-cross thing?' Robert asked. 'Please,' he remembered to say.

'Yes, but be very careful with it. I'd be lost without that gadget.'

Robert squeezed the handles and the finger bits jumped forward so that he could pick up Great Granny's handkerchief with it and wave it under her nose.

'That's the way,' said Great Granny.

Suddenly there was an extra loud crash from the kitchen.

'Oh dear,' said Great Granny.

'It's all right,' Robert said. 'That's just Susan and Daisy.' And then he remembered Rosie and called out, 'Rosie! Come and see. This is Great Granny.'

But Rosie didn't come.

Robert went to the door and looked for her. She was standing at the bottom of the stairs.

'Come on,' said Robert.

Rosie shook her head.

'She won't come,' Robert said to Great Granny. 'She's gone shy.'

'Never mind,' said Great Granny. Then she

called out, 'Good morning, Rosie. Can you guess what my name is?'

'Great Granny,' Rosie called back.

'That's right,' said Great Granny. 'But I've got another name. It's what I was called when I was a little girl.'

Rosie was quiet for a moment. 'Is it Rumpelstiltskin?' she asked. Robert gave a great shout and began to jump around the hall singing, 'This guessing game you'll never win, For my name is *Rumpelstiltskin*. We had that story at play group,' he told Great Granny.

'Then do *you* know what my name is, Robert?' she asked.

So Robert guessed. 'Is it Shagribanda?' he asked.

'No, that is not my name. Do you give up?' Great Granny asked.

'Yes,' said Robert.

'Yes,' called Rosie from the bottom of the stairs.

'Then I'll tell you,' said Great Granny. 'It's *Rosie*.'

And then little Rosie ran across the hall and peeped into Great Granny's room. She had a quick look at Great Granny and then ran away again.

Robert looked at Great Granny. 'She's still shy,' he said.

'Not to worry,' said Great Granny. 'She'll soon get used to me. You go and play with her.'

So Robert went and sat beside Rosie on the bottom stair.

'Don't be frightened, Rosie,' he said.

'Why is she called Rosie?' said Rosie.

But Robert didn't know why either.

Then Rosie gave his arm a little push and pointed to the door of Great Granny's room. 'Look,' she whispered.

A red woolly glove was waving at them around the door of Great Granny's room. It disappeared and then came back again. Then it went away again and a grey furry hat appeared

instead. That went away and a blue handkerchief waved instead. Robert crept forward and grabbed the handkerchief. 'Got it,' he yelled.

Then the red glove appeared again and this time Rosie crept forward and grabbed it. 'Got it,' she shouted too.

When another red glove appeared Robert jumped at it at once. But this time there was a hand – Great Granny's hand – inside the glove and it grabbed him instead.

'Aah, save me! Save me!' Robert shouted and Rosie ran to save him. She caught hold of Robert around his middle and pulled. Great Granny let go and – bump – Robert fell backwards on to Rosie who fell backwards on to her bottom.

'Oh, my goodness!' said Great Granny looking around the door of her room. 'What a heap of children.'

But Robert and Rosie laughed and stood up. 'I saved him,' said Rosie.

'You did indeed,' said Great Granny. 'We are strong women – us Rosies.'

Rosie nodded. 'My Daddy says I'm as tough as an old boot.'

'Do you know,' said Great Granny, '*My* Daddy used to say much the same about me – and he was quite right.'

Leg Trouble

Robert and Rosie played on the stairs while Great Granny finished getting dressed. They jumped down one stair to the bottom. Then they jumped down two stairs. But when Robert tried to jump down three stairs he landed with such a bump that he hurt his leg. He wanted to cry but decided not to because he thought his mother might be cross about the jumping.

So Rosie said, 'Never mind. Let's go and see Great Granny.'

Robert hobbled over to the door of her room and pushed it open. Then he screwed up his face and said in his saddest voice, 'I hurt myself.'

'Oh, catastrophe!' said Great Granny folding her nightdress neatly. 'Where does it hurt?'

'My leg. It hurts.' And Robert nearly began to cry after all.

'That's funny,' said Great Granny. 'Mine does too. How are yours, Rosie?'

Rosie came into Great Granny's room. 'Mine's

all right,' she said. 'I didn't try jumping three stairs.'

'Ah, I *see*,' said Great Granny looking at Robert.

'It's better now,' said Robert quickly. 'Can I show Rosie that criss-cross thing – please?'

Great Granny nodded and Robert took the gadget off her bed and picked up one of Great Granny's slippers with it.

Great Granny smiled at Rosie, 'Where do you live, dear?' she asked.

Rosie pointed out of the window. 'There,' she said.

'Just next door!' said Great Granny.

'Yes,' Rosie nodded. 'But I used to live in London.'

'Well, fancy that,' said Great Granny. '*I* live in London.'

'Do you live in a flat?' Rosie asked.

'Yes, that's right, I do. Did you?'

'Yes, we lived five floors up. Right up high,' said Rosie.

'Good heavens!' said Great Granny. 'I only live three floors up.'

'I liked the lift best,' said Rosie. 'My brother used to go up and down, up and down until my Mum got fed up. She likes it best here. We've just got stairs now.'

'I wish we had a lift,' said Robert. 'I'd like to go up and down, up and down.'

'Yes, it's fine while a lift is working. But sometimes they break down and that's a catastrophe for me,' said Great Granny.

'Oh, cat-as-trophe,' said Rosie very carefully.

'Yes, oh catastrophe,' said Great Granny. 'Can you think why?'

Robert thought. 'You can't go upstairs. Your legs don't work well any more.'

'That's right,' said Great Granny. 'I remember one week last winter. I put on my hat and coat, slung my bag around my neck, picked up my two sticks, locked up my front door, pressed the button to make the lift come and – nothing happened.'

Rosie looked hard at Great Granny's legs. 'Can they go *down* stairs?' she asked.

'No,' said Great Granny. 'They won't go up-stairs and they won't go downstairs. Aren't they stupid!'

Rosie went over to stand beside Great Granny. 'They go forwards and backwards,' she said.

'They go sideways too,' said Robert.

Great Granny laughed. 'You're quite right, they do. So I went backwards into my flat again. And then something lovely happened.'

'What?' Rosie asked.

'Well, do you remember the lady who lives in the next flat to mine, Mrs Hargreaves?'

Robert nodded. 'I gave her Great Granny's key,' he explained to Rosie.

'That's right,' said Great Granny. 'And she has a kind daughter called Clare. And when Clare found out about the lift not working she came and said she would do my shopping for me. And that's what she did. She went and bought bread and butter and some bananas and cheese. She isn't very much older than you but she carried everything up the stairs for me. When she got back we had a special tea and Mrs Har-greaves came in too and it *was* jolly. And since then Clare often does some shopping for me.'

'Do you always have a special tea?' Rosie asked.

'Quite often,' said Great Granny, 'and I make flapjacks.'

'Can *we* make flapjacks?' Robert asked. 'I like flapjacks.'

'Well, I have another plan. But I'll have to ask your mother about it,' said Great Granny. 'But, in the meantime, shall I tell you what I'd really like to do?'

'Yes,' said Robert and Rosie together.

'I'd like to go outside into the garden. How about that?'

'We'll come too,' said Rosie. 'Can we go shopping for you as well – like Clare?'

'That is really kind of you,' said Great Granny. 'But you're a little bit too young to go out by yourselves, aren't you?'

Rosie nodded. And then she had an idea. 'If you come too, you can look after us,' she said.

So Robert went to tell his mother in the kitchen what they were doing. And Great Granny put on her hat and coat, slung her bag around her neck and picked up her sticks. Rosie put on her coat and Robert put on his duffle coat. Susan and Daisy came to the front door with Robert's mother to wave goodbye.

Very slowly Great Granny and Robert and Rosie walked down the road to the village shop.

Sometimes Robert walked backwards and sometimes he walked sideways. There was lots of
time because Great Granny could only walk very
very slowly indeed.

When they reached the shop Great Granny
bought two big jars of mincemeat, some butter
and lard and a bag of flour. The kind man in
the shop who was called Mr Barrett put the
shopping in two bags so that Robert and Rosie
could carry it. Then he said, 'Happy Christmas,

madam,' to Great Granny and 'Happy Christmas, rascals,' to Robert and Rosie.

And Robert and Rosie shouted, 'We wish you a merry Christmas and a happy New Year,' because they had learnt to say that at their play group.

'And the same to you,' said Mr Barrett. Then he went to a sack by the door of the shop and fetched out two big carrots. He gave one to Rosie and one to Robert. 'Those are for the reindeer,' he said. 'Put them on your doorstep on Christmas Eve – and don't forget. A carrot will keep them going till they get to me.'

Mince Pies

After lunch Robert's mother and Great Granny had a cup of coffee and Robert and Susan watched Bagpuss on the television.

Great Granny said to Robert's mother, 'Would it be all right if Robert and I made the mince pies this afternoon, dear? We bought the stuff this morning.'

'That would be a great help, Granny,' said Robert's mother thankfully. 'I must wrap up some presents. I can do it while Susan has her rest.'

'Trific-trific-trific,' shouted Robert, who had been listening as well as watching. 'Can I go and get Rosie?'

'Is that all right?' Robert's mother asked Great Granny.

'Yes, run around and fetch her,' Great Granny said to Robert. 'I don't think I've ever had a friend called Rosie before. Though my friend Mary had a doll called Rosie, now I come to think of it, but that wasn't at all the same.'

A little while later Robert came back with Rosie.

'My mum says I can stay for as long as you want,' said Rosie.

'Marvellous,' said Great Granny. 'I'll get a lot of work out of you. Now, first of all, you both put on aprons and then we all wash our hands.'

Robert used Great Granny's criss-cross gadget to get the aprons off the hook on the kitchen door. He had never been able to reach the hook before. 'I wish *I* had a gadget like this,' he said.

'Perhaps you will when you're ninety,' said Great Granny.

Great Granny tied the strings of the children's aprons for them and Rosie did up Great Granny's apron behind her back.

'Now, we're ready,' said Great Granny sitting down in a chair. 'I shall tell you what to do. Rosie, get the kitchen scales out of the cupboard. Robert, get the mixing bowl and pie tins. Quick, quick!'

Rosie tried to lift the scales. 'They're too heavy,' she said.

'Help her, Muscles,' Great Granny said to Robert.

And, between them, Robert and Rosie heaved the scales on to the kitchen table and got out the other things.

Great Granny put the butter and lard they had bought on the flat tray of the scales. 'Now, Rosie,' she said. 'You get a big spoon and spoon flour into the other side of the scales until both sides go up and down.'

'It's called balancing. I weigh things at play group,' said Rosie, spooning on the flour.

'Out with the rolling pins, Robert,' said Great Granny. 'Flour into the mixing bowl, Rosie, and then measure as much flour again. Now, Robert, are you good at counting?'

'Sometimes,' said Robert.

'Could you count twelve spoonfuls of cold water?' asked Great Granny.

'He forgets about eleven,' said Rosie. 'Eleven twelve, dig and delve.'

'I don't forget,' said Robert.

'Yes, you do,' said Rosie.

'You just do it,' said Great Granny. 'If you two squabble I'll be after you with a rolling pin.'

'My mum says "with a wooden spoon",' said Rosie.

Great Granny pointed sternly at the scales and Rosie got on with spooning out the flour and Robert climbed on a kitchen stool to turn on the cold tap. Then he put the spoon under the water and – *splash* – cold water shot all over him.

'Turn the tap off. You'll drown us,' called Great Granny.

Robert reached over and twisted the tap – the wrong way. Water bounced into the sink and splashed all over Robert, the kitchen and Rosie, who came to help him.

Robert tried again and this time turned the water down to a trickle.

'Phew,' said Great Granny, wiping water off herself and the table with a drying-up cloth. 'That's one way to clean the kitchen.'

Robert carefully began to fill the spoon and tip the water into the measuring jug, counting as he did so. Rosie counted too in case he forgot eleven. But he didn't.

Meanwhile Great Granny chopped the butter and lard into little bits and tipped it into the flour. 'Now,' she said, 'get rubbing, lady and gentleman. Roll up your sleeves and rub in those lumps of butter and lard.'

So Rosie and Robert rubbed the lumps into the flour. They rubbed and they rubbed until Rosie said, 'I'm puffed.'

'Very well,' said Great Granny. 'Now, Robert. Pour in the water and stir with that plastic spatula.'

Robert poured in the water and Rosie stirred. 'That's the way,' said Great Granny.

'It looks yucky,' said Rosie.

'Does it?' said Great Granny. 'Push the bowl over here.'

Robert pushed it across the table and Great Granny squeezed the pastry together with one hand. She squeezed and tossed, squeezed and tossed and, in no time at all, she held up a great big round ball of pastry. 'We forgot to put in the salt,' she said.

'My mum says we mustn't eat too much salt,' said Rosie.

'Oh, well,' said Great Granny. 'Worse things

happen at sea.' And she cut the big ball of pastry into four lumps. 'Get rolling,' she said. 'A bit of flour on the table and roll away.'

Robert used his own small rolling pin and Rosie used his mother's big one. Then they swapped over in case the other one was easier. Robert's pastry stuck. It stuck to his rolling pin. It stuck to his fingers and it stuck to the table. Rosie's didn't.

'How about you doing the mincemeat filling and I'll take over the rolling?' Great Granny suggested.

Robert nodded and rubbed his hands together to get the pastry off.

Rosie cut out the bottoms of the pies with a big cutter. Great Granny cut out the lids with a

smaller cutter and put the circles of pastry into the tins. Robert spooned in the mincemeat.

They worked and they worked and when it was getting dark, and Robert had to switch the light on, Great Granny said they had made forty-eight mince pies.

'That's even more than twenty,' said Rosie.

'It is indeed,' said Great Granny. 'We'll cook some now and put some in the freezer on top of the fridge. And Robert, can you find three clean spoons? It's time for cook's perks.'

'What's cook's perks?' asked Robert.

'It's a prize for whoever's done all the work. And that's us.'

And Great Granny scraped around the inside of the mincemeat jars. 'There you are,' she said passing a mincemeaty spoon to Rosie, 'here's a perk for you, and another for Robert and another for me. How about that?'

Rosie flopped down on the floor and licked her spoon.

'I'm ready to drop,' she said.

'No dropping,' said Great Granny, 'until after we've done the washing-up.'

Robert and Rosie groaned.

'Ah,' said Great Granny, 'don't forget about the washer-upper's perks.'

'What's that?' asked Robert, brightening.

'A mince pie, of course,' said Great Granny.

Some time later when all the washing up was done and Rosie had wiped the table with a big damp cloth and Robert had wiped the floor, Great Granny got a tin of mince pies out of the oven.

'We must let them cool down a bit,' she said and felt behind her back to undo her apron. 'Rosie,' she said, 'what have you done to my apron strings?'

'I'm not very good at bows,' said Rosie.

'But you're *very* good at knots,' said Great Granny. 'I'm done up like a Christmas parcel.'

Parcels

The next morning Robert woke up and sat up. It was very dark. 'It's Christmas Eve,' he thought and scrambled out of bed. He ran across the bedroom floor and opened the door. Very quietly he ran downstairs and went and knocked at Great Granny's door.

'Eh?' said Great Granny.

Robert pushed open her door and went inside. 'It's Christmas Eve,' he whispered.

'Eh?' said Great Granny again.

'There's a lot to do today. We'd better wake up,' said Robert.

'What time is it?' Great Granny asked.

'I can't tell the time,' said Robert.

Great Granny looked at her clock which shone in the dark.

'It's not yet six o'clock,' she said and reaching across she turned on the light beside her bed. 'Where are your slippers?' she asked.

'Upstairs,' whispered Robert.

'I can't hear you,' Great Granny whispered back. 'My ears don't work well. They are rather old.'

Robert nodded. 'If I get into bed beside you,' he said in a louder voice, 'you'll be able to hear me.'

'Get in then,' said Great Granny, shifting over a little in her bed. 'Aah,' she said as Robert got in, 'your feet are like icicles.'

'They're all right now,' said Robert. 'They can warm up on your legs.'

Robert snuggled up beside Great Granny. 'Did you have Christmas Eve when you were little?' he asked.

'Every year,' said Great Granny. 'And it's the best day of the year too,' she added.

'I've got to go and get the Christmas tree today with Daddy,' said Robert. 'We'll put up holly and I'm going to wrap up parcels. I've got Susan an ice-lolly. It's in the freezer.'

'How are you going to wrap that up?' Great Granny asked.

'It's got a wrapper on already,' Robert explained. 'What did your brother George give you when you were little?' he asked.

Suddenly he felt Great Granny begin to shake and he looked up quickly. Great Granny was laughing. 'Earth,' she said.

'Earth?' said Robert. 'That's not a present.'

'That's just what I said too,' Great Granny said. 'I remember that bad boy running in from the garden and shouting, "Rosie, Rosie, come quick. Your Christmas present's in the shed." Well, I was out of the house like a lamplighter and I rushed down the garden to the shed and pulled open the door and there – there, on the bench, was a lovely big parcel, all done up with Christmassy red paper and string. *"Thank you,"* I said and went over to unwrap it. It was very heavy and difficult to move to get the string off, I remember, but I managed it and pulled back the paper and there was a load of lumpy earth

from the flower bed. Most of it fell off the bench all over the floor of the shed. And George stood in the doorway and laughed. He was *doubled up* with laughter.'

'What did you say?' Robert asked.

'I didn't say anything. I kicked him,' said Great Granny. 'My legs worked *very* well in those days. And then I went back indoors leaving him to clear up the mess. He didn't, of course, and Father got cross with him later in the day. And I was not a bit sorry for him, not a bit. But I did laugh later because Father found a little note among all the spilled earth. It said, "Add water to make mud".'

'Yes, I can do that,' said Robert.

'But I'm afraid it gave us a bad idea,' Great Granny went on, 'and might have got us into trouble. You see, one of us had the idea of playing the same trick on other people.'

'Was it you or George?' Robert asked.

'I can't remember – it's so long ago. But, anyway one of us did. And when we were friends again we went out into the garden and wrapped up three big parcels of earth. It was quite difficult getting the string around them. Then we tied them with bows so that they would undo easily. And we took them down to the lane that ran along the side of our garden. We put one down by the edge of the lane and went

and hid behind the garden hedge.'

'Then what happened?' Robert asked.

'Nothing, for a long time. I got very cold and was just going indoors when old Mrs Appledore came down the lane taking her pug dog for his afternoon walk. She stopped and she peered at the beautiful parcel all done up in red and green paper. She prodded it with her stick and the pug dog sniffed at it carefully. Then she bent down very slowly and stiffly and pulled the bows undone. I began to giggle and had to stuff my handkerchief into my mouth to smother the noise. But I expect she was as deaf as I am now because she didn't seem to hear. She pulled the parcel open and out tumbled a load of earth. "Bah," she said and pushed the parcel on to the grass at the side of the road. "Come along, Marco," she said to her dog. "It's just stupid tricksters – pay no attention," and off she went down the lane.

· 'Well, we waited until she was out of sight and then ran around the end of the hedge and cleared up Mrs Appledore's parcel and put another in its place.

'We didn't wait long this time. Along came Mary's father.'

'Was he in his car?' Robert asked.

'He was indeed,' said Great Granny. 'And he must have got better at stopping because as soon as he saw the bright parcel he stopped *at once* – screech – and his engine stalled – that means stopped dead. He jumped down and went straight to the parcel. He picked it up and turned it over. But we hadn't made a very good job of wrapping it up, because it began to dribble earth out of one corner. I remember he frowned and looked up and down the lane. Then he shook the parcel and earth *cascaded* out. I burst. I couldn't help it. And Mary's father heard me and, do you know, he *jumped* right over that hedge. It wasn't a very low hedge. It was taller than you are now. But over he went and landed almost on top of George and me.'

'What –?' said Robert, but Great Granny carried on.

' "You scallywags!" he yelled and jumped on us. He began to tickle us. We shouted and wriggled and tried to get away but it was no good. He tickled and tickled until I felt quite weak. And then Mother came out to see what all the noise was about. Mary's father saw her coming and we were saved. You see, it wasn't long since Mother had been so cross with him about my car ride. So he touched his hat, said "Good afternoon" and jumped back over the hedge. But, of course, he had to crank and crank the starting handle of his car before it would go. I remember Mother stood and watched him. "A strange man," she said as she took us indoors and I'm afraid we didn't tell her it was all our fault. We were just very glad that it hadn't been Mrs Appledore who found us out. Then we *would* have been in trouble.'

'What happened to the last parcel?' Robert asked.

'I think George got rid of it. Anyway, he didn't try to trick anyone else with it. But I always opened his presents carefully after that – just in case.'

Robert nodded. 'I think we'd better start getting up now. There's lots to do,' he said.

'All right,' said Great Granny. 'But no parcels of earth, mark you. Or *I'll* be in trouble!'

Johnny Jones's Christmas

Robert's father was at home all Christmas Eve. He and Robert's mother had a lot of work to do. Robert went with him to fetch the Christmas tree and a big box of fruit and vegetables from the greengrocer's shop in the village. Then they went down the garden and planted the tree in a large flower-pot.

'You smell that tree,' Robert's father said. 'It's one of the great Christmas smells.'

Robert's father was very happy while he got the box of tree decorations out from the cupboard under the stairs. But then he started to test the electric fairy-lights to see which ones were working from last year, and he stopped being so happy. He started being rather cross, so Robert let Susan through into the hall to keep him company and went to find his mother instead.

He found her looking in her cookery books and frowning over a bag of chestnuts. Great

Granny was sitting at the kitchen table peeling Brussels sprouts.

'How many of us will there be for Christmas lunch?' Great Granny asked.

'Ten, I think,' said Robert's mother. 'There are five of us in the house and Granny and Grandad, Grandma and Grandpa and Uncle Frank. Yes, ten.'

'Are those chestnuts worrying you?' Great Granny asked.

Robert's mother laughed. 'Yes, they are. I haven't made chestnut stuffing before,' she said.

'No problem,' said Great Granny. 'That can be a job for Robert and me this afternoon.'

Suddenly the kitchen door opened and Susan came in, crying.

'Can't she stay in here?' said Robert's father. 'She keeps getting under my feet.'

As he said this the back door opened and Rosie appeared.

'I've finished helping at home,' she said, 'so I've come to help you.'

Robert's mother looked at Great Granny.

Great Granny said, 'Run away, Rosie, but come back this afternoon after the washing-up's done. Robert and I need you to help with the chestnuts. Now, run!'

'See you later,' said Rosie cheerfully and ran.

'See 'oo later,' said Susan, just as cheerfully,

and walked back into the hall to help her father.
At that moment all the electric fairy-lights began
to work again, so Susan was allowed to stay.

That afternoon Great Granny, Robert, Susan
and Rosie took the large baking tin full of cooked
chestnuts into the sitting room out of everyone's
way. Great Granny had a sharp kitchen knife,
Robert and Rosie had a teaspoon each and Susan
had a plastic bowl.

Great Granny put three warm chestnuts in
Susan's bowl for her to play with while she and
the other two children got down to work.

'Now,' said Great Granny, 'I'll slit the chestnuts open and I want you to dig out the insides

with your spoons. Put the nuts in this saucepan and the shells on the newspaper.'

'Can we have cook's perks?' Rosie asked.

'We'll see,' said Great Granny.

'Can you tell us about the olden days?' Robert asked.

'Yes, yes,' Rosie shouted. 'Tell me about Johnny Jones, your donkey. Robert told me about him.'

'Then you know all about him,' said Great Granny.

'No,' Rosie shook her head. 'Tell me *all* about him. And about George.'

For a while Great Granny cut open chestnuts and handed some to the children. Then she stopped and said, 'Are you sitting comfortably? Then I'll begin. When I was a little girl my grandmother used to come and stay with us at Christmas. And she used to tell us Christmas stories. One of the best ones was about the animals talking on Christmas Eve. Though they were dumb all the year long, on Christmas Eve they were able to talk. It was the animals' special Christmas gift because the ox and the ass and the lambs had warmed the Infant Jesus when he was born in that cold stable. George used to say, "Tell us about the animals talking. Tell us again." And our kind grandmother did – again and again.

'Well, I remember one Christmas Eve George and I hung up our stockings by the fireplace on the hooks that the poker and tongs usually hung on. Our father put out a glass of whisky for Father Christmas and Mother put a mince pie on the mantelpiece.'

'Did you put out a carrot for the reindeer?' Robert asked.

Great Granny shook her head. 'I'm afraid we quite forgot about the reindeer,' said Great Granny.

'I shan't,' said Rosie.

'Of course not,' said Great Granny. 'But anyway, off I went to bed – early I think, so that the morning would come more quickly. And then I tried to go to sleep. But I couldn't. The more I tried the more awake I felt. Well, George couldn't sleep either and he came to my bedroom and whispered, "Let's go and talk to the ass." "What ass?" I asked. "Johnny Jones, of course," he said. "An ass is a donkey. So Johnny Jones is an ass. And he ought to be talking by now, shouldn't he?" "That's just a story," I said. "Well, I'm going to find out," said George. And off he went. I got up and followed him downstairs. The house was very quiet. We unbolted the back door and went out to Johnny Jones's stable. I'm sure we didn't have a light, so I expect the moon was out. I can remember

how Johnny Jones's white coat seemed to glow in a very special way. "Sit down," George said to me. "Let's listen." So we sat in the straw on the floor of Johnny Jones's stable and waited for him to talk. We stared at Johnny Jones and he stared at us. Sometimes his ears would twitch, but he didn't say a thing. George had a lovely Cox's apple which he had taken off the fruit dish in the dining room, and he gave the donkey that. And then, believe it or not, we heard a funny rumbling sound.'

'Eeee,' said Rosie.

'George looked at me. "I think it's coming from *inside* him," he said. And he put his ear against the side of Johnny Jones's hairy, fat, soft tummy. I put my ear against his other side. But all I could hear were funny gurgling, rumbling noises – no talking at all. But George said, "I heard something, I did," in such an excited way that I tried again. "He said '*Scarper*'," George whispered. "He did – you listen." "What does 'scarper' mean?" I asked. George sighed and said, "You don't know anything, do you? It means 'go away'. It's what they say in London." So I tried to hear it, but really I thought George was making it up. At last I said, "If that's what he wants, let's scarper." And we stood up to go back indoors. But as we left Johnny Jones's stable our cat ran out of the house and down to the stable. "I expect he's going for a chat," George said. We crept indoors and bolted the back door behind us.'

'What was the cat's name?' Rosie asked.

'Thomas,' Great Granny replied. 'But Father called him "Cat". And as we crept down the hall to the stairs we saw the fire glowing where we had hung our stockings. All of a sudden George grabbed my arm. "The whisky's gone," he said. And, do you know, *it had*. There was an empty glass on the mantelpiece and no mince pie either. "There's something in our stockings," said George, and we ran into the room and yes, it was true, our stockings were so full

there were presents falling out of them on to the floor. My word, we were excited. "This is why Johnny Jones said 'scarper'," said George. *"He wanted us to find the presents."* And in no time at all we had pulled off all the wrapping paper and were having a lovely time. I remember George had some soldiers he'd wanted very much and I had lots of lovely little zoo animals – wooden ones. I kept them for years. But we made such a racket that, of course, Mother and Father heard us and came downstairs. I looked up and saw Father standing in the doorway. "Father Christmas has been," George shouted. "Johnny Jones told us." And Father said, "Johnny Jones has no business telling you such things. It is still

Christmas Eve." And then Mother appeared in the doorway holding a little present. She gave it to Father and said, "Cat told me Christmas is starting early this year." And she gave him a kiss. Father kissed her back and said he had better have a drink to keep Father Christmas company, if Christmas was really starting early.'

'Did you take your toys to bed with you?' Robert asked.

'I *think* so,' said Great Granny. 'And I remember our grandmother came out of her bedroom, so George told her about Johnny Jones saying "scarper" to us. And she said she would go and have a chat to him herself. But I don't know if she ever did.'

'Susan's eating the chestnut shells,' Rosie said. 'I'll try talking to my hamster tonight.'

'If you're sensible, you'll go to bed early,' said Great Granny.

'And *I* won't forget about the reindeer,' said Rosie.

Christmas Morning

Robert ran downstairs. Then he turned and began to run upstairs again. Susan would want to see her stocking, he thought. But then he remembered that she would need her nappy changing, and he ran downstairs again.

There were the stockings lying on the mat in front of the sitting room fireplace. They were bulging with presents. And there were *three* of them. Last night Robert had hung up his and one for Susan, but now there were three. He looked at the extra red stocking and saw a label on it. Two letters were on the label – two big gees. Robert picked up his stocking as well as the red one and carried them through the hall to Great Granny's room.

Great Granny's light was on.

'I thought I heard somebody get up,' she said. 'What have you got there?'

'This is mine,' said Robert happily, 'and this is somebody else's.'

Great Granny leant forward and looked at the label. 'My goodness me,' she said. 'Those gees stand for Great Granny. *Kind* Father Christmas!'

And Robert and Great Granny began to rip off paper and laugh and look and laugh again.

'Don't be too noisy,' Great Granny warned. 'Grown-ups like to sleep a bit longer.'

So after that Robert buried his face in Great Granny's eiderdown when he wanted to laugh. 'I've got a pencil case for when I go to school,' he said.

'I've got some new handkerchiefs for when I blow my nose,' said Great Granny.

'I've got some Lego men,' said Robert.

'I've got some lemon soap,' said Great Granny.

Then, Robert remembered. 'Wait here,' he said. 'I've got a present for you in the kitchen.'

'Go quietly,' said Great Granny.

Soon Robert was back. In his hand was a beautiful red and black ice-lolly. 'I took off the wrapper for you. You can have it now.'

'Oh, Robert, you *are* a generous boy,' said Great Granny.

'It didn't cost much. Mr Barrett let me have it cheaply because he'd had it a long time. Do you like it?' Robert asked.

'It's lovely,' said Great Granny. 'You have a lick.'

Robert licked the ice-lolly while Great Granny went and fetched her criss-cross gadget from beside her suitcase.

'Now,' she said. 'You feel about under the bed with this and see if you can catch anything.'

Robert gave the ice-lolly back to Great Granny and took her gadget. He squeezed the handles and out shot the picking-up fingers. Then he knelt down and pushed it under Great Granny's bed. 'There's something there. Got it!' he said. He pulled the gadget back and there was a parcel done up in purple and orange paper.

'It's for you,' said Great Granny.

'It's not earth,' said Robert quickly.

'No, it's not earth,' Great Granny laughed. 'You look.'

Robert pulled at the sticky tape and opened one end of the parcel. He looked inside. He could see a little black shiny thing. Then he pulled the paper back a bit further and saw a black and white stripey face. He looked up at Great Granny and laughed. 'It's that badger from the shop. Thank you, thank you,' he said.

'Not at all,' said Great Granny politely. '*Somebody* had to rescue him.'

Robert pulled all the paper off the little badger and gave him a hug. 'He can have a happy Christmas with Panda,' said Robert.

'No more being squashed by that great pink teddy,' said Great Granny. 'What are you going to call him?'

Robert looked at his badger and stroked him gently. 'Can I call him Johnny Jones?' he asked.

'What a good idea,' said Great Granny. 'I'm sure no badger was ever called that before.'

'And he can come to church with me,' said Robert. 'Susan and me put the straw in the crib at church.'

'Did you really?' said Great Granny. 'Where did you get it from?'

'From Mr Mummery's – where the donkey lives,' said Robert. 'He let us have it all free. We put it in big plastic bags. Blue ones. Mr Mummery has a great pile of blue bags.'

'Was it heavy?' Great Granny asked.

'No – yes,' said Robert. 'But I did carry it all the way to the church.'

'Phew,' said Great Granny.

'I pulled my bag over my shoulder like Father Christmas,' Robert explained. 'Mummy carried the other one.'

'That was a lot of straw,' said Great Granny. 'Where did you put it?'

'Susan and me – we put it round the place where the babies are christened,' said Robert. 'Mummy had to go and fetch Mrs Armitage, you see.'

'Oh,' said Great Granny.

'And Susan put it on the benches too,' said Robert.

'Why?' said Great Granny in a very interested voice.

'I *think* it was for the people to sit on. I'm not sure. But Mrs Armitage picked it all up again. I helped too.'

'Where should it really have gone?' Great Granny asked.

'In the side place, Mummy said. And only a little. Then Susan got lost,' said Robert.

'Oh dear,' said Great Granny.

'We got her back because she yelled and screamed. She's not quiet in church,' said Robert.

'Where was she?' Great Granny asked.

'She was under the cupboard. She got out the hymn books and got under the cupboard. Mummy pulled her out. Then we came home.'

'What happened to all the straw that was left over?' Great Granny asked.

'I carried it,' said Robert. 'Then we gave it to

Rosie's hamster. It keeps him warm.'

'Well, I shall look forward to seeing the crib at church,' said Great Granny.

'I'd better take Susan that stocking,' Robert said.

Great Granny nodded. 'Yes, you could now,' she said. 'I heard someone moving upstairs.'

'And I'll give Mummy her present,' said Robert.

'What have you got for her?' Great Granny asked.

'One sock,' said Robert.

'*One* sock?' said Great Granny.

Robert nodded. 'Susan's got to give her the other one because Daddy forgot to get a present for her to give.'

'I see,' said Great Granny. 'Well, thank you for the lovely lolly and thank you for the story. I'll get dressed just as soon as I've finished this lolly. And you wish everybody a happy Christmas from me.'

Pass-the-Parcel

After church on Christmas morning Robert was playing with a new garage beside the Christmas tree when there was a loud knock at the front door.

'They're here,' he shouted.

'Merry Christmas,' said a voice through the letter box.

'It's Grandad,' Robert yelled and tried to open the front door.

'Give it a shove,' called Grandad and suddenly the door flew open and there were Granny and Grandad.

Everybody hugged everybody else and Granny picked up Susan to stop her being trodden on. Then there was another loud knock at the front door and Robert managed to open it again. This time it was Grandma and Grandpa and Uncle Frank.

'Now we can have lunch,' Robert shouted. But they didn't. First, they all gave each other presents. And soon the house was full of bits of wrapping paper. Robert's father said he would have a grand bonfire that evening.

Uncle Frank gave Robert a big book about trains and Granny gave him a navy blue jumper which she had knitted herself.

Great Granny had to sit down to open all her presents because she needed both hands. Robert leant her sticks against the mantelpiece in the sitting room and helped her pull the sticky tape off her presents. One present was a very heavy box. 'It's from James, your Grandad,' she said. 'Whatever can it be?'

'It's jars,' said Robert pulling back the paper. 'It's jam. It's damson jam!'

'That's right, Robert,' said Grandad.

'Did you make it yourself?' Robert asked.

Grandad *was* pleased. 'That's right,' he said. 'Imagine remembering that.'

'Great Granny told me about damsons,' Robert explained. 'But I don't think they're bad luck.'

'Just as well,' whispered Grandad. 'I'm giving some to your mother as well.'

'Can we have some of your marmalade too – please?' Robert asked. 'You make very good marmalade.'

'Dear me,' said Grandad. 'I'll have to make a lot extra this coming year. I didn't know my marmalade was *famous*.'

After that Robert ran back to play with his garage and found Uncle Frank was playing with it already. 'This is a real bobby-dazzler,' said Uncle Frank in the way he did when he was pleased about something, and he whizzed one of Robert's little cars down the sloping road of the garage.

'I'm sitting next to you at Christmas lunch,' Robert said.

'Then no pinching my sprouts,' said Uncle Frank sternly. 'That's what you did when you were Susan's age.'

'Oh,' said Robert, quite surprised.

After the grown-ups had had a drink of sherry

and Robert had some apple juice it was time for the Christmas lunch.

Robert's father had pushed two tables together in the dining room and Susan sat on Granny's knee because there wasn't space for her high chair.

'James must sit beside me,' said Great Granny, 'where I can keep an eye on him.'

'I will if I can pull a cracker with you – and keep the inside,' said Grandad James.

Robert's father carved the turkey and Robert's mother passed around dishes of roast potatoes, bread sauce, sausages and bacon rolls, sprouts and cranberry sauce.

'What a feast,' said Great Granny. 'No, James! Don't take my sprouts, you naughty boy.'

'Susan only wants the cranberry sauce,' said Granny.

'I can eat the rest for her,' Robert said. 'The chestnuts are the best bit.'

'Look, there's a reindeer,' called out Uncle Frank staring out of the window.

Robert turned to look out of the window. There was nothing there. When he turned back all his sprouts had gone. 'Hey!' he shouted, looking at Uncle Frank and laughing.

'I am *very* fond of sprouts,' said Uncle Frank.

'That's no excuse,' said Grandma, who was Uncle Frank's sister. 'Give them back, at once.'

'No, it's all right,' shouted Robert happily. 'I've just taken his chestnuts.'

'Now then, you two,' said Robert's mother. 'No more bad tricks or there'll be no pudding.'

'*No pudding*?' said Uncle Frank. 'We'll be good.'

But while Uncle Frank was looking at Robert's mother, Robert took one of Uncle Frank's roast potatoes off his place. Uncle Frank didn't notice. Then Robert found he had too many potatoes and he put it on Granny's plate on the other side of him. But she was talking so much that she didn't notice either. Robert looked at Great Granny and she winked at him.

'It's getting like pass-the-parcel,' she said to Robert. He laughed and the other grown-ups looked sharply at Great Granny and Robert.

'Somebody is up to bad tricks,' said Robert's mother. 'And I can guess who.'

'Who? Who?' shouted Robert.

'Great Granny,' said Robert's mother.

'Well, what a thing to say,' said Great Granny. 'Just when I'm eating up like a good girl. Whatever next!'

'Not to worry, Mother,' said Grandad James. 'You'll grow out of it.'

'*You* never did,' laughed Robert's father.

'Now, now. It's time to pull our crackers,' said Robert's mother. 'Or there'll be *no pudding*, remember.'

Everybody picked up their crackers at once.

The crackers were very good ones. Grandma had brought them as an extra present. Susan had a bright pink paper hat with silver trimming. But she pulled it down over her face and began to yell. 'There, there,' said Granny waving the pretty bead necklace out of her cracker in front of Susan. 'Don't cry on Christmas Day, sweetheart.' But Susan began to cry even harder.

'It's time she had a rest,' said Robert's mother.

'I'll put her up in her cot,' said Granny.

'And I'll fetch the mince pies,' said Robert's father.

Robert had to sit up very straight to eat his mince pie. He felt very full of good lunch.

'These are a bit of all right,' said Uncle Frank. 'Excellent, in fact.'

'You must thank the young gentleman sitting beside you for these,' said Great Granny proudly.

'What?' said Grandad James. 'Did you make these pies, Robert?'

Robert nodded because his mouth was full of mince pie.

'Well, well,' said Grandad. 'I had better have another, hadn't I?'

Robert swallowed and nodded again. 'There are lots more in the freezer. I can get some more.'

'No – no more,' said Great Granny. 'Or James will eat too much – and pop.'

'Bad luck, old boy,' said Grandpa to Grandad James. 'Bad luck.'

'Bad luck!' Robert shouted, even though his mouth was full of mince pie again. 'It's that damson jam – that brings bad luck.'

'Oh well,' said Great Granny. 'Just *one* more, James. We can't have bad luck on Christmas Day.'

Teeth

On Christmas Day evening Great Granny went to bed at the same time as Robert. She said she was tired and bed was the best place to be.

Robert came downstairs in his pyjamas to say goodnight to her.

'Is that little sister of yours *still* crying?' Great Granny asked.

Robert nodded. 'It's her tooths – teeth,' he said. 'Her face goes all red and she yells and gets cross. Mummy says she'll be all right when the tooth comes. But then she has another one.'

'Oh dear,' said Great Granny. 'What a trouble these teeth are.'

'Daddy says –' Robert began, looking hard at Great Granny's face, 'Dad says you can take your teeth out and put them back in again.'

'Does he indeed?' said Great Granny. 'Well, yes, I can. They're called false teeth because they aren't real – they are false.'

'Can I see you take them out?' Robert asked.

'No,' said Great Granny.

'Oh,' said Robert, disappointed.

Then Great Granny said, 'Has your father told you about how he found out about false teeth?'

'No,' said Robert, 'you tell me.'

'Well,' said Great Granny, 'when your father was a boy he used to come and stay at my house quite a lot. And one time when he came to stay with us he had a wobbly tooth.'

'I know,' said Robert. 'Rosie's big brother has wobbly tooths and when they come out he puts them under his pillow and the fairies give him ten pence. I try to make mine wobble. But they won't,' he added.

'They will,' said Great Granny. 'Just you wait a year or so and then they'll wobble beautifully. Well,' she went on. 'When your father came to stay with us he was about a year older than you are now and his bottom front tooth was wobbling nicely. And one day, when he had an apple for supper, out it came and stuck in his apple. He *was* pleased. And my husband –'

'Great Grandfather Robert,' said Robert.

'That's right. Well done,' said Great Granny. 'You are getting to know us all, aren't you? Well, Great Grandfather Robert said, "You'll have to put that under the carpet in your bedroom, young man. The fairies will give you real silver for that."

'Did they?' Robert asked.

'Of course,' said Great Granny. 'We wrapped it up in a piece of white paper and put it under the carpet in the corner of his bedroom. And in the morning it had gone. In its place was a silver sixpence. That was a lot of money in those days.'

'Lucky Dad,' said Robert.

'Mmmm,' said Great Granny, but she shook her head and pursed her lips.

'What happened next?' Robert whispered.

'I'll tell you very quietly,' said Great Granny, 'because I'm afraid your father was not a good boy in this story.'

Robert sighed.

And Great Granny sighed. 'The next morning your father got up early and went into the bathroom before anybody in the house had got up. And there, on the bathroom shelf, were your Great Grandfather Robert's false teeth. They were sitting in a glass of water in the way they always did during the night. And your father saw all those false teeth and thought what a lot of sixpences the fairies would bring him if he put all those under the carpet.'

Great Granny shook her head sadly.

'So he took them out of the glass, I'm afraid, and he pushed them very quickly under the nearest carpet he could find and he ran back to bed to wait for the fairies to come. But fairies aren't stupid, are they?' said Great Granny.

Robert shook his head.

'They know false teeth aren't real teeth, and they didn't come at all. But I did. I got up as usual at seven o'clock and went downstairs. And as I went across the landing carpet I trod on the bit at the top of the stairs and something went

crunch under my foot. "Whatever's that?" I thought. And I bent down to pull back the edge of the carpet and there were –'

'Great Grandfather's teeth,' Robert whispered.

And Great Granny nodded and began to laugh and Robert jumped on to the end of her bed and they both laughed.

'What's all the noise about?' asked Robert's father, looking around the door of Great Granny's room. 'What are you two up to?'

'We were just talking about teeth,' said Great Granny.

'Oh?' said Robert's father.

'And false teeth and fairies,' said Great Granny.

'Oh,' said Robert's father and he grinned. 'I thought I would make a fortune. And if your Great Granny hadn't trodden on them, Robert, I'd have got a great bag of money.'

Robert shook his head. 'Fairies aren't stupid,' he said and pursed his lips in the way Great Granny did.

'Bed-time – at once,' said his father sternly.

The Last Story

On Boxing Day morning – the morning after Christmas – Robert went into Great Granny's room to help her eat her breakfast. Her suitcase was open on the chair and her skirts and blouses were neatly folded inside it.

'Why is that there?' Robert asked.

'I'm going home this afternoon,' Great Granny said.

Robert said nothing for a moment. Then he said, 'I didn't know you were going.'

'Well, I have been here a week,' said Great Granny. 'I've had a lovely Christmas and a lovely rest. But it's time to go home.'

'Oh,' said Robert glumly.

'Can you help me to pack?' Great Granny asked.

'Yes,' said Robert.

'Thank you, dear,' said Great Granny.

Robert picked up a pair of Great Granny's shoes and put them in the suitcase.

'Cheer up,' said Great Granny. 'Shall I ask your father if you can come with us when he takes me home?'

'Yes, please,' said Robert in a small voice. He put Great Granny's slippers in her suitcase and said in a louder voice, 'Can we have some flapjacks when we get there – please?'

'Yes, indeed,' said Great Granny. 'I think there were some left.'

'Yes, there were six left. I put them back in the tin with the castle picture on top,' said Robert.

'Excellent,' said Great Granny. 'That's one for your father, one for you and four for me.'

'No, no,' said Robert, nearly laughing. 'Six for me, you mean.'

'Oh, do I?' said Great Granny. 'Have you got any space left in your tummy after yesterday's great meal?'

'Yes,' Robert nodded.

'Then here you are,' Great Granny said. And she handed him a piece of bread and marmalade.

Great Granny finished her packing during the morning. Robert helped her to pull all the sheets and blankets off her bed and fold them up. He liked doing that. He stood at one end of the room and held two corners of the sheet and Great Granny stood at the other end and held

the other two corners. When she put her corners
of the sheet together he did the same at his end.
Then he ran up to her and put his end of the
sheet into her hands and picked up the middle
that flopped on to the floor.

'I like this,' he said.

'I do too,' said Great Granny, putting the

neatly folded sheet on the end of the bed. 'But it's a difficult job to do by yourself.'

After lunch Robert's father drove the car out of the garage and put Great Granny's brown suitcase into the boot. Great Granny kissed Robert's mother and thanked her for her happy visit. Then she kissed Susan and told her to be good.

'Some hope of that,' said Robert's father.

'Some 'ope,' said Susan.

Then Robert's father helped Great Granny into the front of the car and put her sticks in beside her. Robert belted himself in at the back.

As they drove off Robert waved to his mother and Susan. His mother waved back and blew him a kiss. Susan tried to do the same. She was still trying when the car turned the corner and Robert couldn't see her any more.

'That was one of the best Christmasses I've had,' said Great Granny. 'And I've had a lot.'

When they arrived at Great Granny's flat Robert knew which button to press in the lift without being told.

Mrs Hargreaves had turned on the heating in the flat and put some freesia flowers in a vase on the mantelpiece. They made the whole flat smell lovely.

'Ah!' said Great Granny, smelling the flowers. 'It's good to go away and it's good to come back.'

Robert went into the kitchen to look for the tin with a picture of a castle on it.

Robert's father put down Great Granny's suitcase and said, 'I'll just nip along to the shop at the corner, Gran. I can get any food you need to keep you going. And you can put the kettle on.'

'That *is* kind of you, dear,' said Great Granny. 'A pint of milk and a loaf of bread, if they've got any left, please. That'll do fine.'

So Robert's father went back down in the lift and on down the road to the shop.

Great Granny walked slowly, slowly into her kitchen and plugged in her shiny electric kettle.

'There's nothing like a cup of tea,' she said.

When the kettle boiled she made a pot of tea and put it on the table to brew. Then she sat carefully down in her special chair with strong arms so that she could get out of it easily.

'Ah,' she said again in a contented way.

'Can we have another story, now, before Daddy comes back?' Robert asked, holding the castle tin against his chest with one arm and pulling off the lid.

'Let me think,' said Great Granny. 'Yes, do have one. They are there to be eaten.'

Robert helped himself to a flapjack.

'Now then. This is a story of not very long ago. Nearly five years ago – five years ago next spring. Well, one morning I woke up and the flat was full of sunshine. The daffodils in the window boxes were waving a little in the breeze and the trees in the park on the other side of the road were showing little green leaves. It was a lovely morning. I got up and made my breakfast and thought, "Today is such a wonderful day I must go for a walk in the park." A very slow walk, of course, and anyway perhaps that's the best kind of walk. So I put on my hat and coat –'

'And put your bag round your neck,' Robert said.

Great Granny laughed, 'No, I didn't,' she said. 'I didn't because, just as I was going to, the telephone rang. And who do you think it was?'

'Who?' said Robert.

'It was your father. He said, "Good morning, Gran. It's a boy." "*What*?" I said. "When?" And he said, "He was born this morning and he's a whopper – eight and a half pounds. And how does it feel to be a Great Granny?" "It feels *wonderful*," I said. "Wonderful and marvellous. What are you going to call him?" And he said, "Robert James."'

'*Robert James*?' said Robert. 'That's *my* name. That was *me*. I was born.'

'Well, there you are,' said Great Granny. 'And that's how I heard you had been born and how I heard you were a whopper.'

'What did he say next?' Robert asked.

'Well, he told me that you and your mother were very well and then I told him to stop talking because he had lots of other people to telephone. He had to tell your Granny and Grandad and your Grandma and Grandpa.'

'And Uncle Frank,' said Robert.

'Yes, of course. So I put down the telephone and then do you know what I did?'

'No,' said Robert.

'I stood and looked out of the window and the sun was even brighter and the daffodils were even yellower. And then I *did* hang my bag around my neck and I went out of the flat, down in the lift and along the road to the wine shop. And there I bought some bottles of sherry wine. The kind man who works there said he would carry them up to my flat. Oh, and I bought some cheesy biscuits as well.

'Then back home I went and pressed the lift button to go up to the very top floor. My friends David and Jane live up there and they had a baby girl called Alice. I rang their bell and asked them to come to a party at mid-day in my flat. Then I went down to my floor and asked Mr and Mrs Hargreaves and Clare, who was about four then, to come too. And Mr Hargreaves went down to the flats below and asked the Dixons and the Williamses to come as well.

'And at mid-day – that's twelve o'clock – everybody came into my flat and Mr Hargreaves opened the bottles of wine and Clare opened the packets of cheesy biscuits. We all had a glass of wine –'

'Did Clare?' Robert asked.

'Perhaps she had a sip, because it was, after all, such a *very* special day.

'You see, dear, I had been a Granny for years and years and had got quite used to it – very

used to it. But then you were born and you made me a Great Granny which, of course, is far better. So I raised my glass and said, "Here's to Robert James, my great grandson." And everybody else raised their glasses too –'

'Did Clare?' Robert asked.

'Certainly – if she had one,' said Great Granny, 'and they all said, "Here's to Robert James" as well.'

Robert was very pleased to think of all the people in Great Granny's flat saying, "Here's to Robert James," and he sat and thought about it while Great Granny poured out three cups of tea.

Then they heard Robert's father coming back into the flat and Robert ran around the kitchen table and gave Great Granny a hug. 'I'm very glad I made you a Great Granny,' he said.

'Well, do you know,' said Great Granny, 'so am I.'

You can see more Magnet Books
on the following pages:

ANNE ROOKE

When Robert Went To Play Group

When Robert first goes to play group he
feels rather shy, but he soon makes friends,
especially with Hector the large ginger cat.
He discovers how much fun play group is
– and despite setbacks like a broken arm
and catching chicken pox, he and his new
friends find lots to enjoy, particularly when
the group go on an outing for a train ride!

These delightful short stories are warm,
funny and real and are ideal for reading
aloud to pre-school children.

SAM McBRATNEY

Colvin and the Snake Basket

Colvin finds life as piggy-in-the-middle
between sister Beccy and baby 'Lamb
Chop' full of difficulties. His best laid plans
and favourite games always seem to end in
trouble and disaster. But when life gets too
much for him, he can always go into
hiding – in the snake basket along with the
laundry!

TONY BRADMAN

Dilly the Dinosaur

Dilly is the naughtiest dinosaur in the
whole world. There was the time he
decided he wasn't ever going to wash
again. Another day he decorated his
bedroom using his sister's best painting set.
And when he doesn't get his own way, he
opens his mouth and lets loose his ultra-
special, 150-mile-per-hour super-scream!

Dilly's Muddy Day

Further adventures of the world's
naughtiest dinosaur. Dilly goes to the park
and rides his dino-trike into the swamp!
He even tries to open his own shop to
make more pocket money!

Illustrated by Susan Hellard

ANDREW DAVIES

The Fantastic Feats of Doctor Boox

What would *you* do about a giraffe with a
sore neck?
Or ducks that sink?
Or the slowest greyhound ever seen?
Don't know?

Then send for Doctor Boox, the greatest
animal doctor in the world!

By the author of *Marmalade Atkins*.

BEL MOONEY

I Don't Want To!

Kitty's favourite word is NO! She doesn't
want to clean her teeth or wash or eat her
vegetables or – worst of all – play with
boring cousin Melissa. But saying no gives
Kitty more problems than even *she*
bargained for – and somehow she always
ends up wanting to say yes!

Illustrated by Margaret Chamberlain

MARGARET GREAVES

Charlie, Emma and Alberic

Charlie, Emma and the Dragon Family

Charlie, Emma and the School Dragon

Charlie and Emma haven't got a pet – they have to make do with the neighbourhood cat. Then one day they find a tiny dragon down a hole in the road. Of course, Alberic wants to go home with them – and that's just the beginning of their adventures together . . .

Illustrated by Eileen Browne

More Fiction from Magnet Books

While every effort is made to keep prices low, it is sometimes necessary to increase prices at short notice. Magnet Books reserve the right to show new retail prices on covers which may differ from those previously advertised in the text or elsewhere.

The prices shown below were correct at the time of going to press.

All these books are available at your bookshop or newsagent, or can be ordered direct from the publisher. Just tick the titles you want and fill in the form below.

MAGNET BOOKS   Cash Sales Department
P.O. Box 11, Falmouth,
Cornwall TR10 9EN

Please send cheque or postal order, no currency, for purchase price quoted and allow the following for postage and packing:

UK	60p for the first book, 25p for the second book and 15p for each additional book ordered to a maximum charge of £1.90.
BFPO & Eire	60p for the first book, 25p for the second book and 15p for each next seven books, thereafter 9p per book.
Overseas Customers	£1.25 for the first book, 75p for the second book and 28p for each subsequent title ordered.

Name (Block letters) ....

Address ....

....